'Night, Mother Goose

Library of Congress Cataloging-in-Publication Data
Bernal, Richard.
'Night, Mother Goose / by Richard Bernal.
p.   cm.
Summary: A child at bedtime bids good night to favorite Mother
Goose characters.
ISBN 0-8092-4305-9
[1. Bedtime—Fiction.   2. Books and reading—Fiction.]   I. Title.
II. Title: Goodnight, Mother Goose.   III. Title: Good night, Mother
Goose.
PZ7.B4548Ni   1989
[E]—dc20   89-32770
                                                        CIP
                                                         AC

*The artist dedicates this book to
Friedrich and Marie Messmer.*

Published by Contemporary Books, Inc.
180 N. Michigan Avenue, Chicago, Illinois 60601
Manufactured in the United States of America
Library of Congress Catalog Card Number: 89-32770
International Standard Book Number: 0-8092-4305-9

Published simultaneously in Canada by Beaverbooks, Ltd.
195 Allstate Parkway, Valleywood Business Park
Markham, Ontario L3R 4T8 Canada

'Night, Mother Goose

Written and Illustrated by
RICHARD BERNAL

A CALICO BOOK
Published by Contemporary Books, Inc.
CHICAGO • NEW YORK

'Night, Three Blind Mice

*

'Night, Little Bo-Peep

'Night, Old King Cole

’Night, Peter Pumpkin Eater

'Night, Little Boy Blue

'Night, Jack Sprat and Mrs. Sprat

'Night, Humpty-Dumpty

'Night, Old Woman in the Shoe

'Night, Mother Goose

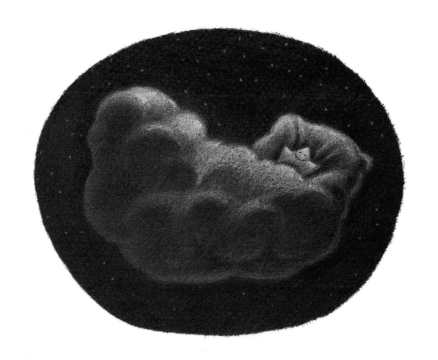